17.96a

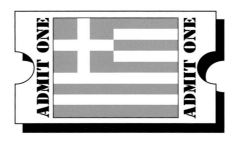

Boaters Near
A Windmill
On Paros
Island

FACES
AND
PLACES

GREECE

BY PATRICK RYAN

THE CHILD'S WORLD ®

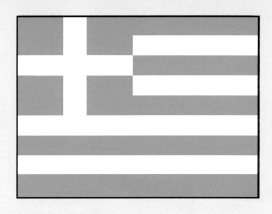

COVER PHOTO

A little girl on the island of Rhodes.
©Dave G. Houser/CORBIS

Published in the United States of America by The Child's World®
PO Box 326
Chanhassen, MN 55317-0326
800-599-READ
www.childsworld.com

Project Manager James R. Rothaus/James R. Rothaus & Associates
Designer Robert E. Bonaker/R. E. Bonaker & Associates
Contributors Mary Berendes, Dawn M. Dionne, Katherine Stevenson, Ph.D., Red Line Editorial

The Child's World® and Faces and Places are the sole property
and registered trademarks of The Child's World®.

Library of Congress Cataloging-in-Publication Data
Ryan, Patrick, 1948–
Greece / by Patrick Ryan.
p. cm.
Includes bibliographical references and index.
ISBN 1-56766-908-5 (lib. bdg. : alk. paper)
1. Greece—Juvenile literature.
I. Title.
DF717 .R93 2003
949.5—dc21

00-011063

Table
of
Contents

CHAPTER	PAGE
Where Is Greece?	6
The Land	9
Plants and Animals	10
Long Ago	13
Greece Today	14
The People	17
City Life and Country Life	18
Schools and Language	21
Work	22
Food	25
Pastimes and Holidays	26
Country Facts	28
Greece Trivia	30
Glossary	31
Index and Web Sites	32

Imagine flying over Earth in the space shuttle. You would see large land areas surrounded by water. These land areas are called **continents.** Greece is at the southern tip of the continent of Europe.

Greece is made up of a mainland and many islands. To the north Greece shares its borders with Albania, Macedonia, and Bulgaria. To the east lies Turkey. Greece's islands lie in the waters of the Mediterranean, Aegean, and Ionian Seas.

Western Hemisphere

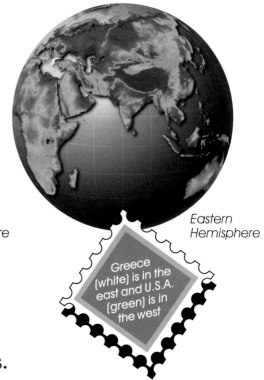

Eastern Hemisphere

Greece (white) is in the east and U.S.A. (green) is in the west

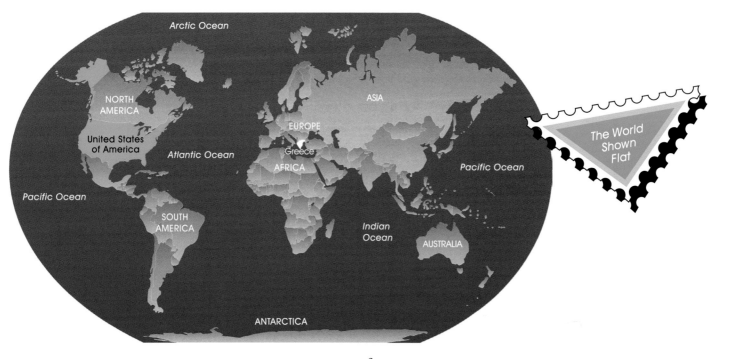

The World Shown Flat

6

BULGARIA

MACEDONIA

TURKEY

ALBANIA

GREECE

Aegean Sea

TURKEY

Ionian Sea

*Mediterranean
Sea*

Farmland On
Crete

THRACE
MACEDONIA
EPIRUS THESSALY
EUBOEA
Isthmus Of Corinth
KHIOS
IKARIA
PELOPONNESUS
PAROS
THIRA
CRETE

©Gail Mooney/CORBIS

Cliffs On The Island Of Thira

©Gail Mooney/CORBIS

Greece is a rugged, dry nation of islands and mountains. It has more than 2,000 islands, but only about 170 have people on them. The major islands are Crete, Euboea (yoo-BEE-uh), Ikaria (ih-KAR-ee-uh), and Khios (KEE-ohs). Crete, the largest island, supports a population of over half a million people.

About 80 percent of Greece's mainland is mountainous. It can be divided into three sections. The northern section includes Thrace and Macedonia. Epirus (ih-PY-russ), Thessaly, and Central Greece make up the middle section.

The Old Port Of Skaia On Thira

©Gail Mooney/CORBIS

The Peloponnesus is in the south. The Peloponnesus is a **peninsula** surrounded mostly by water. It is connected to the rest of the mainland by a narrow stretch of land called the **Isthmus** of Corinth.

Greece's rugged landscape, with its land of different heights, supports interesting plant life. Trees that grow on lower land include oranges, olives, dates, pomegranates, figs, and cotton. Trees on higher land include evergreens, oaks, black pine, beeches, chestnuts, and sumac. Wildflowers such as tulips, hyacinths, and laurels grow in Greece's mountain areas.

Greece has interesting wildlife, too. The European black bear still roams the area. So do boars, lynxes, jackals, small antelopes called chamois (SHA-mee), deer, foxes, badgers, and weasels. Hawks, nightingales, turtle doves, and pelicans soar through the skies.

©David Lees/CORBIS

A Pelican Sitting Near The Water

Goats Climbing Rocks On The Island Of Crete

©Gail Mooney/CORBIS

Other common birds are egrets, pheasants, partridges, and storks. In the seas, dolphins and porpoises follow small boats. The waters around Zakynthos (ZAK-een-thahs) are home to Greece's last large colony of sea turtles.

ZAKYNTHOS

CRETE

©Clay Perry/CORBIS

Yellow
Flowers Cover
A Field On
Crete

The Tholos Ruins At Delphi

Delphi

Navarino

Greece has one of the longest histories in the world. More than 3,000 years ago, people were already building societies in many areas of Greece. About 2,400 years ago, the Greeks fought many battles against nearby countries and kingdoms. Soon Greece ruled most of that part of the world. But Greece's power quickly came to an end, as the Romans and then the Turks conquered the Greek empire.

Greece was ruled by the Turks for almost 400 years. The Greek people were unhappy and wanted their freedom. Finally, they fought against the Turks and won their independence in 1828. But Greece was just a tiny part of what it used to be.

Much of Greece's land had been taken over by other countries. Greece worked hard over the years to win back some of its land. Even as recently as 1920, Greece was still working with other countries to gain back some of the lands it had lost.

Greeks Fighting
The Turks In
Navarino
In 1827

©Archivo Iconografico, S.A./CORBIS

World War II brought more fighting and unrest to the country. During the war, Greece's German and Italian enemies wanted to set up military bases in Greece. The Greek leader, Joannes Metaxas, said "Ochi!" "Ochi" means "No." Every October 28 is "Ochi Day," a national holiday to celebrate Greece's independence. Greek "resistance" fighters fought the Germans and Italians and helped win the war.

©Dave Bartruff/CORBIS

Greek Guards Marching Outside The Parliament In Athens

In 1975, Greece got rid of its king and adopted a **constitution.** Today Greece has a **parliament,** a president, and a prime minister. The president performs ceremonial duties. The prime minister is the leader of the country. In 1981, a peaceful and united Greece entered the European Community. It is now a partner and active member in this new union of countries.

©Hulton-Deutsch/CORBIS

Greek Soldiers At An Anti-Aircraft Gun In 1940

The
Greek
Parliament
Building In
Athens

A Man
Playing A
Bouzouki
On The Island
Of Rhodes

RHODES

Ano Moulia • • Ageos Nikolaos

Hotel Owners In Ageos Nikolaos

With its many boats and harbors, Greece has always been a seafaring nation, and Greeks have always been a people on the move. Over the years, many Greeks have **emigrated** to other parts of Europe, to North America, and to Australia. Greek restaurants and customs are now found around the world.

©Sheldan Collins/CORBIS

A Shepherd With A Mule In Ano Moulia

Almost all of Greece's people come from the same cultural or **ethnic** background. The rest of the population is made up of small numbers of people from other groups, such as Turks, Armenians, and Macedonians.

©Richard Bickel/CORBIS

ADMIT ONE

City Life
And
Country
Life

ADMIT ONE

The Town Of
Imerovigli
On The
Island
Of Thira

©Gail Mooney/CORBIS

Almost two-thirds of Greece's people live in city, or **urban,** areas. In fact, nearly a third live in the city of Athens. Most Greek cities have both an old section and a modern area. Most city dwellers live in tidy modern apartments. Like many areas of Europe, Greece has a modern mass transit system. Some cities limit the use of automobiles to reduce air pollution.

Traffic In
Athens

©Wolfgang Kaehler/CORBIS

Few Greek people still live on farms. Most people who live in the country live near the sea. Many Greeks own summer homes in their home villages. They live in the city but return to the villages on holidays.

★Athens

•Imerovigli

•Canea

©Gail Mooney/CORBIS

The Hellenic Academy In Athens

Hydra

★ Athens

Gytheio

©Paul Almasy/CORBIS

A Gym Class Exercising In Gytheio

©Farrell Grehan/CORBIS

Going to school in Greece is much like going to school in the United States. Children begin school when they are 6 years old. Students learn math, reading, and writing, just as you do. Greek children may leave school when they are 15 years old, but many go on to one of Greece's universities, colleges, or technical schools.

A Painted Sign In Hydra

TABEPNA

TA ΔΥΟ ΜΑΣ

©Richard T. Nowitz/CORBIS

Today Greek people use a written language much like the one their **ancestors** used 2,500 years ago. That means that if ancient Greek students could travel to the present time, they could read a modern Greek newspaper!

A Fisherman On A Small Sailboat Near Ithaca

Most Greeks work providing services to other people, in areas such as health care, education, banking, government, and transportation. Many people also work serving the millions of **tourists,** or visitors, who travel to Greece each year.

Workers Restoring The Parthenon In Athens

One out of every five people in Greece works in manufacturing. Greece's factories produce everything from chemicals and cement to beverages, clothing, and footwear. Greek farmers work hard, too. Their farms produce crops such as oranges, peaches, potatoes, sugar beets, and tobacco.

©Kevin Fleming/CORBIS

A Woman
Milking A
Goat Near
Ithaca

Ithaca
★Athens

A Man Selling Vegetables In Hydra

Thessaloniki

Hydra

Irakleio

©Dave G. Houser/CORBIS

ΠΑΡΑΛΙΚΑΚΗ
Λ-20

400

Olives For Sale At A Market In Thessaloniki

©Vanni Archive/CORBIS

Many of Greece's foods are combinations from cultures that ruled the country long ago. Many dishes have Turkish backgrounds, such as a yogurt dip called *tzatziki*. Other favorite dishes include *moussaka* (baked eggplant with meat sauce) and *souvlaki* (meat, onions, and tomatoes served on a long stick).

A Fresh Produce Market In Irakleio

©Gail Mooney/CORBIS

Greeks eat lamb more than any other meat. They also enjoy using the country's famous feta (FET-uh) cheese in many recipes. Greek olives are used in everything from salads to breads. Greeks also love the many types of seafood that come from the nearby Mediterranean Sea.

A Woman At A Celebration Near Thessaloniki

Greeks love sports. In fact, the Olympic Games started in Greece more than 2,200 years ago! The games were originally part of a religious festival. Instead of gold medals, the winners were crowned with olive leaves. Most Greeks today enjoy two sports above all others—soccer and basketball. Greece's major cities have professional teams that play against each other.

Greeks celebrate many of the same holidays Americans do. Easter is the most important holiday. The day before Easter season begins, people celebrate with feasts and a big party called a carnival. Greeks celebrate Christmas, but they do not exchange presents. Instead, people share presents on Saint Basil's Day, January 1.

Greek Folk Dancers In Rhodes

Greece is a fascinating country with a long history. Maybe you will visit Greece someday. If you do, be sure to see the old buildings the ancient Greeks built—and appreciate the people who built them so long ago!

©Charles & Josette Lenars/CORBIS

Mount Olympus +

Thessaloniki

Piraeus ★ Athens

Rhodes

A Greek
Orthodox
Religious
Ceremony
In Athens

Area
About 50,950 square miles
(131,940 square kilometers)—slightly smaller than Alabama.

Population
About 11 million people.

Capital City
Athens.

Other Important Cities
Thessaloniki (theh-suh-loh-NEE-kee), and Piraeus (py-REE-uss).

Money
The drachma (DRAK-muh).

National Sport
Soccer.

Official Name
Hellenic Republic.

National Song
"Hymn to Liberty."

National Flag
Nine stripes of blue and white, with a blue square and a white cross in one corner. The cross stands for the Greek Orthodox religion.

Highest Mountain
Mount Olympus, which is 9,570 ft (2,917 meters) high.

The Moon
Over The
Parthenon
In Athens

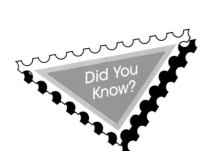

The first Greeks were stargazers. Their stories about the heavens named the groups of stars we call **constellations.** The early Greeks also created stories about their gods that we still know as Greek **mythology.**

About 2,500 years ago, Greece won a battle at a place called Marathon. News of the victory was carried to Athens by a runner. Today's marathon races are named after that run.

A giant statue called the Colossus of Rhodes was one of the Seven Wonders of the Ancient World. At its finished height, the statue was about 120 feet (37 meters) tall—a little smaller than the Statue of Liberty. Unfortunately, the Colossus of Rhodes collapsed in an earthquake shortly after it was built.

Today visitors can still see the ruins of ancient Greece's beautiful buildings. The Parthenon in Athens lies atop a flat hill called the Acropolis. The Parthenon is one of the wonders of Greece's golden age.

How Do You Say?

	Greek	*HOW TO SAY IT*
Hello	gia'sou	YAH-soo
Goodbye	andi'osas	ahn-DEE-oh-sahs
Please	parakalo'	par-ah-KAH-loh
Thank You	efharisto'	eh-far-ee-STOH
One	e'na	EH-nah
Two	di'o	THEE-oh
Three	tri'a	TRREE-ah
Greece	Ellada	el-LAH-dah

ancestors (AN-sess-terz)
Ancestors are members of someone's family who lived a very long time ago. Greek people use a written language much like the one their ancestors used.

constellations (kon-stel-LAY-shunz)
A constellation is a group of stars that seem to form a shape, such as a person or an animal. Many constellations, such as Cassiopeia and Orion, were named by the Greeks.

constitution (kon-stih-TOO-shun)
A constitution is a system of laws for a country. Greece adopted its constitution in 1975.

continents (KON-tih-nentz)
Continents are huge areas of land that are surrounded mostly by water. Greece lies at the southern end of the continent of Europe.

emigrated (EM-ih-gray-ted)
Someone who has emigrated has left one country to live in another. Many Greeks have emigrated to other parts of Europe.

ethnic (ETH-nik)
When something is ethnic, it deals with cultures or languages that people have in common. Almost all of Greece's people come from the same ethnic background.

isthmus (IS-muss)
An isthmus is a narrow neck of land that extends through water to connect two land areas. Greece has an isthmus called the Isthmus of Corinth.

mythology (mih-THOLL-oh-jee)
Mythology is a group of stories (called myths) that express a people's set of beliefs. Hercules and many other famous story characters come from Greek mythology.

parliament (PAR-luh-ment)
A parliament is a group of people who make laws for a country. Greece's parliament, president, and prime minister all work together to make laws for the country.

peninsula (peh-NIN-soo-lah)
A peninsula is a land area surrounded by water and attached to land on only one side. The Peloponnesus in southern Greece is a peninsula.

tourists (TOOR-ists)
Tourists are people who visit other places to sightsee and travel. Many tourists go to Greece.

urban (UR-ben)
Urban is having to do with a city or living in a city. Most Greeks live in Greece's cities, or urban areas.

Index

animals, 10
cities, 18, 26, 28
Colossus of Rhodes, 30
constellations, 30
constitution, 14
continents, 6
country life, 18
crops, 22
education, 21, 22
emigration, 14
ethnic background, 17
European Community, 14
factories, 22
foods, 25
government, 14, 22, 28

history, 13, 14, 26
holidays, 14, 18, 26, 28
housing, 18
independence, 13, 14, 28
islands, 6, 9
isthmus, 9
land, 6, 9, 10, 13
language, 21
location, 6
marathon, 30
Metaxas, Joannes, 14
mountains, 9, 10
mythology, 30
Ochi Day, 14

Olympic Games, 26
parliament, 14
Parthenon, 29, 30
pastimes, 26
peninsula, 9
people, 9, 13, 14, 17, 18,
        21, 22, 26, 28
plants, 10
Romans, 13
sports, 26
tourists, 22
transportation, 22
Turks, 13, 14
World War II, 14

Web Sites

Learn more about Greece!

Visit our homepage for lots of links about Greece:
http://www.childsworld.com/links.html

Note to Parents, Teachers, and Librarians:
We routinely verify our Web links to make sure they're safe,
active sites—so encourage your readers to check them out!